SHENANIGANS IN THE SHADOWS

KARI LEE TOWNSEND

OLIVER
HEBER
BOOKS

To my first born, Brandon. This is the year you graduated high school and headed off to do amazing things in college. I can't wait to watch you play lacrosse and hear about all of your grand adventures. No words can describe how proud I am of the man you have become. It was so hard to let you go, but you made it easier just by seeing how excited and happy you are. As a mother, that's all I can ask for. Thanks for all of your help over the years in brainstorming my stories, and don't think this means you are done. Love you kiddo!

1

———

"Here we go again," I said, staring at my big white cat, Morty. He stood defiantly in front of the window in my ancient Victorian house in Divinity, New York, casting a foreboding shadow behind him. A telling smirk crossed his aristocratic face as he shot me a parting look with his jet black eyes and then walked regally out of the room.

"What do you mean?" asked my best friend and proud owner of Smokey Jo's Tavern, Joanne Burnham, swiping burgundy curls over her voluptuous shoulder and studying me with curious, smoky gray eyes.

"Punxsutawney Phil's *six more weeks of winter* has got nothin' on Mischievous Morty's *six more weeks of doom*. The look in his eyes just now said it all. Frankly, I can't take any more shenanigans from either of them. If they don't knock it off, I'm building a doghouse and putting them both in it!"

"I take it things still aren't going well between him and Detective Stone?"

"They seemed to have called a sort of truce. I just never dreamed that asking Mitch to move in with me would cause so much chaos. Morty doesn't exactly like to play nice in the sandbox. This end of summer heat wave isn't helping matters any, either." I slicked back my short blond hair, praying for a breeze to blow in through the open window. My old house didn't have air conditioning, something that Mitch hadn't been happy to discover shortly after moving in a few weeks ago.

"Maybe Morty's jealous of the attention you're giving to Mitch instead of him now that you're finally a *real* couple. I just went through that with Cole and Biff."

Biff was the beautiful Great Dane pup Cole and Jo had adopted from Animal Angels recently. Poor baby had been abused, but once Cole laid eyes on him, he was a goner. Biff didn't like to share his daddy with anyone, not even Jo. They had just bought a house with a fenced-in yard in preparation for their wedding and the new family they planned to start soon after.

I glanced outside at Biff lying like an angel in the shade under a tree in the back yard. "What did you do, tranquilize him? He used to be so hyper."

"Nah, he's a good boy. I just had to let him know who the boss was."

"Yeah, well, easier said than done with Morty, considering the house is his and he was gracious enough to let *me* stay. He's his own boss, and we all know that."

"I wasn't talking about Morty." Jo's eyes sparkled.

I laughed over that one. "You might be onto something."

"Speak of the devil." Jo grinned as my big brooding hulk of a man Mitch walked through the front door, followed closely by her even bigger tattooed, leather covered Sasquatch Cole. Morty shot outside before the door closed, and Mitch grunted as if to say *good riddance*, then the men joined us in the living room.

He frowned at Jo while rubbing his whiskered jaw,

the scar that graced it and his crooked nose. "I can only imagine what you two were talking about." Then he looked at me and arched a thick black brow, the crease on his forehead deepening. I wasn't about to tell him. Let him worry for a change. Lord knew he and Morty had certainly put me through enough worry as of late.

"Did you put the rings someplace safe?" I asked.

"I'm a cop, *Tink*." He winked, tossing around my nickname to tease me. He slapped his chest. "I'm the king of safety."

Cole's grandmother had recently died, leaving him her gorgeous set of heirloom wedding rings stored in an antique hand-painted box to give to Jo. He was all his grandmother had left, except for an estranged cousin they never saw, so she'd wanted him to have something special to give to the angel who'd saved his life after his first wife had died.

Cole's best man was Jo's bartender Sean O'Malley. Sean was working closely with Jo's cousin, Zoe, who was the wedding planner and Sean's date. He was a blond haired, blue eyed, ladies' man with dimples to die for and one of my best friends. Loved the guy, but no way was he responsible enough to hold onto the rings, so they'd asked me. As Jo's maid of honor, the only job I gave Mitch was to guard the rings with his life. A simple, fitting job for a detective.

If I could get him to stop messing around with Morty and focus, that is.

"And where exactly would that 'safe place' be, *Grumpy Pants*?" I asked, throwing his nickname at him, minus the wink. I was so *not* in a teasing mood these days. He was the king of something all right, but safety wasn't the word that came to mind after the way he'd behaved this morning with Morty.

He lost his smile, knowing I wasn't happy with him, and said seriously, "They're in the garage on my new workbench. No one goes in there but me. They're safer there than anywhere. I promise." His eyes softened as he studied me and said in a deep husky voice, "I got this, babe. You can trust me."

I couldn't help melting a little and forgiving him just a tiny bit. "Where's Granny Gert?" I asked with a lot less irritation, changing the subject.

"She took off in that big white Cadillac of hers to run some errands in town," Cole interjected. "She said to tell you she made cookies for Captain Grady Walker and had to talk to the Innkeeper about your parents' reservations for the wedding." He shook his buzzed head with a chuckle. "Lord help anyone who gets in her way."

Granny Gert had passed her road test with a little *help* from some special brownies, but the whole town knew to clear out of her way when she hit the road. Needless to say she was Big Don's best client down at the autobody shop. Her car insurance had to cost more than her car by now, but there was no taking away her independence.

"Where'd Mitch go?" I asked, just now realizing he was gone.

Jo shrugged. "I'm not sure. I saw him slip away while Cole was talking."

We all stared at each other. No words were necessary. Morty was gone. Mitch was gone. Mischief was bound to happen.

"I got the front," Jo said.

"I'll search the house," I added.

"I'll take the back," Cole finished.

We split up and hurriedly looked everywhere for Morty and Mitch, aka Mischief and Mayhem. I had a sinking sensation I wasn't going to like what I would find. Just as I feared, they weren't anywhere inside the house. When I came back downstairs, Jo had walked back inside through the front door. She looked at me and shook her head, which meant they weren't out front either. That could only mean one thing. They were out back.

"I don't even want to know what they are doing in the back yard," I said.

"How bad can it be?" Jo asked.

Cole suddenly threw open the back door and stepped inside with a dark look on his face. "I found them. You might want to brace yourself before you come out here. Something tells me you're not gonna like what you see."

Jo walked past him and stopped in the doorway, clapping a hand over her mouth, her eyes opening wide.

I couldn't take it anymore. I had to see what all the fuss was about. Charging past them both, I ran into the yard and skidded to a stop, my jaw falling wide open. Mitch and Morty stood there, covered in mud and staring at me with guilty expressions. The yard now sported a million holes, giving a whole new meaning to aerating, and all of my flowers had been way more than pruned. They were pitiful. Meanwhile, Biff still sat under the shady tree like the good boy that he was. Jo walked over to him and patted his back, while Cole headed out front to give us some privacy, no doubt.

"That's it!" I shouted to the filthy culprits. "You're both in the dog house until further notice."

"I can explain," Mitch said. "When Morty didn't come back inside, I just knew he was up to no good. And sure enough I found him out here digging up your rose bushes with all these holes in the yard. I tried to catch him and make him stop. That's how I got so dirty myself."

Morty hissed at him, and then just blinked at me, looking down his nose with distaste as if daring me to take Mitch's side over his.

"I'm done with excuses." I swiped my hand through the air, too frustrated and angry at both of them to even think about sides. I adored them each for their own unique qualities, but they were making my life miserable. If they couldn't learn to get along somehow, then I honestly didn't know what I would do. All I knew for sure was that none of us could go on the way things were right now. "Please clean up this mess." I rubbed my temples and counted to ten. "How can I have Jo's wedding shower here with you two screwing everything up?"

"Jo's wedding shower is the least of our worries," Cole said gravely as he reappeared from the front of the house. "The wedding's on hold for the time being."

I gasped. "What?"

"Why?" Jo asked with a shaky voice, looking ready to cry.

Cole met Mitch's eyes and angrily said, "Can't have a wedding without rings, now can we?"

"What are you talking about?" Mitch asked confused and clearly frustrated. "The rings are fine. I put them away myself."

"Call it a hunch, but something made me check the garage." Cole sighed heavily before dropping the bomb, "My grandmother's wedding rings are missing."

2

"I can't believe someone broke into the garage while we were all a few yards away right inside," Jo said later that day while pouring me a beer as I sat at the rich mahogany bar in Smokey Jo's Tavern. She bit into one of the cookies Granny had made me bring to cheer her up and sighed as her eyes rolled back in her head in pleasure. According to my grandmother, there was a cookie for everything.

"I know. It's crazy." I snagged a cookie for myself, took a bite, and tried not to moan. I had to admit Granny's amazing cookies really did make the world a better place.

"It's insane, and yet ingenious because they got away with it." Jo dimmed the lights. Amber lighting cast the perfect ambiance as seventies folk music played softly in the background. The lunch crowd was long gone as she and Sean got ready for the dinner hour. Work had been the perfect therapy for Jo after getting so upset earlier, while Cole had taken Biff and gone to work at the construction site to burn off his anger and frustration.

"Mitch always says most burglaries happen in broad daylight and sometimes even while the people are home," I responded and then took a much needed sip of the draft before me. I still felt horrible about the priceless heirloom rings going missing on my watch. "I can't believe someone would have the nerve to go through with something like that."

She shook her head, and her ponytail bounced. Her lips trembled, but she bit them hard. After a minute, she said, "Those rings were all Cole had left of his family."

"*You're* his family now." I reached out and squeezed her hand. "Don't worry, Jo. Mitch feels awful. He won't rest until he fixes this." He and Jo had been close friends long before I ever came into the picture. Not to mention he was a great detective. If anyone could figure out what happened, Mitch could.

"I know." She took a deep breath and got back to work, talking as she wiped the counters. "I thought he said nothing was missing except the rings? It just looked like someone scratched the door while trying to unlock it, then they must have figured out it was already unlocked and went inside. Then they trashed the place."

"He called his partner Fuller, and they're looking for prints or any other clues that might shed some light on what happened. But I think you just hit on something important," I said, scrunching my brow while I pondered the clues. "The robber trashed the place, yet nothing was missing *except* the rings. It's almost as if the person went there specifically looking for those rings. Like whoever did this knew you were bringing them over today."

Detective Stone might be a good cop, but that didn't mean I couldn't do my own thing, especially when this particular mystery affected my best friend. After helping to solve three different crimes recently, I had begun to trust my instincts. And right now they were telling me I was onto something.

Jo stopped wiping the bar and looked at the ceiling as though trying to recall some incriminating detail. Finally she said, "I have no clue who could have known about the rings Cole planned to give me, let alone that they are priceless heirlooms."

"Sure you do, lass." The blond-haired, blue-eyed hottie with killer dimples, Sean O'Malley, sauntered through the kitchen door, carrying a big crate of clean glasses to restock the bar. His Kelly-green, snug-fitting, T-shirt read: *I'm Irish: Kiss me for luck!*

"What are you talking about?" Jo asked, throwing a towel over her shoulder and hanging the glasses from the top of the bar.

"Remember the phone call Cole got yesterday from his cousin, Diana?" Sean refilled the napkins and salt and pepper shakers while he talked.

"You mean the crazy woman he hasn't spoken to in a decade?" Jo snorted, rolling her eyes.

"That would be the one. I remember Cole wasn't too pleased with her. She didn't bother to come to the funeral or have anything to do with their grandmother in years, yet she felt entitled to those rings after their grandmother passed. That's a wee bit selfish I'm thinking. His grandmother had a soft spot for you, and Cole has always been close to her, never leaving her side at the end. It's only fitting the rings go to you and not her."

"Thanks Sean," Jo gave him a quick hug, "but what does that have to do with what happened today?"

"Only the fact that Cole told her in no uncertain terms she couldn't have the rings. That they were being held in a safe place by a trusted friend. It's not too hard to figure out who that trusted friend is, given that Sunny is your maid of honor and I'm his best man. Hell, even I didn't trust myself with them. I'm the one who told him to give the rings to Sunny. Diana only lives two hours away. She could have easily come to town and tracked Sunny down."

"You know, you're not as dumb as you look," Jo said teasingly, smacking him with her towel.

"Dumb enough to let this lass slip away from me," he said, winking at me. "Right love?"

"Oh, please. If I hadn't said no to you, then you never would have met an even better lass in Zoe. You'd do well not to screw that one up, Romeo."

Ever the flirt, he replied, "I wouldn't say she's a better lass, just better for me in that she hasn't learned to see through me yet."

"On the contrary, my friend." I met his gaze with a knowing look and a wink of my own, "I think she's seen exactly through to who you really are, and that scares you to death."

His charming smile slipped a bit, and he cleared his throat. "I think those spirits have gone straight to your head. Better be careful before you lose your mind completely."

"And you'd best be careful before you lose your heart for *real* this time."

"Touché, I fold. Time to get back to the kitchen since it's getting a bit hot out here." He backed toward the kitchen, waving his hand in the air while carrying the empty crate with his other.

"Chicken," I called after him, to which he clucked and flapped his arms all the way out the back door.

"Do you think he could be right?" Jo asked, looking wide-eyed and shocked. "I mean, they're family."

"They're related, not family. There's a difference,

and trust me, money can make the crazy relatives come out of the woodwork. I think it's worth checking into." I flipped my phone open and dialed the detective.

"Detective Stone here," came the deep voice I adored through my cell, but I squashed the impulse to sigh. He still had a lot of making up to do for contributing to our first experience as a couple being so stressful. I knew everything wasn't going to be perfect after he moved in, but I never expected the degree of difficulty both he and Morty would cause. They needed to worry a bit, because if we were ever going to work, something had to give and soon.

"Hi, Detective. Sunshine Meadows here. Anything new?" I kept my tone formal and my words all business.

"Sunny, come on, now, I—"

"You have news for me? That's wonderful. Just what I hoped for."

"Not quite." He sighed, sensing this wasn't the time or place, no doubt. "No prints other than all of ours, and nothing else missing. Just one big mess and missing rings. This person knew how to cover his tracks, that's for sure. There's not even a hair or fiber from clothing."

"Can you check into something for me?" I asked.

There was a hesitation on the other end of the line. "Okay, shoot."

"Can you see if a Diana West came to town last night or early this morning? Any records at all from hotels, bus stations, train stations, restaurants, etc."

"Can I ask why?"

"You owe me. Isn't that reason enough?"

"Fine. But you're not going to do anything stupid are you?"

"Gee, that's the pot calling the kettle black. Call me back when you get any information, okay?"

"Yes, and for the record...I'm sorry, for everything."

"I know." I finally relented a bit, but added, "Just give me some time to get over being mad." I hung up before I had to either tell him the truth, knowing he would stop me, or have to lie to him, which no matter how mad at him I was, I didn't want to do. Because the truth was I didn't know what I was going to do. I just knew I couldn't sit around and do nothing when my best friend's happiness and future hinged on discovering the truth. And discovering the truth was something I did best.

3

"You are so predictable," said a deep male voice from behind me.

I jumped out of my skin and whirled around, wide-eyed, all in one motion. "Mitchel Stone, you are not funny! Don't do that to me again." I poked him hard in his rock-solid chest and stared up at him. *Way* up since he towered over my five-foot-four-inch frame.

"I'm not trying to be funny." He caught my hand in his much larger one, lines of frustrations etching his rugged face. "I'm trying to save your scrawny behind from going off half-cocked as usual and putting yourself in danger."

I pulled my hand from his and waved it in the air. "Oh, please. I'm perfectly safe. I just decided a night out might clear my head."

"At the Song Bird—a Japanese karaoke bar known for catering to outsiders." He snorted. "Yeah, I'm not buying it." He crossed his muscular arms and stared me down suspiciously.

"Lucky for you I'm not trying to sell anything." I inspected my nails. "Besides, Cole and Jo are supposed to meet me here. You know how Cole loves this place.

And for your information there hasn't been a murder, so the only thing I'm in danger of is—"

"You didn't ask me to join you, even though we're living together?" His tone made my gaze snap to his. "You must really be mad," he added quietly, looking a little dejected and disappointed.

"It's not like that," I quickly replied, placing my hand on his forearm. "I needed a night out alone. You know I care about you, but you and Morty are driving me crazy with all the fighting."

He took my hand in his own and intertwined our fingers, studying them as he replied, "I'm trying, Tink. I really am. That cat hates me."

I sighed and squeezed his hand. "He doesn't hate you. I think he's just jealous. We'll figure something out. Just...try harder."

"So, does your night out alone involve hoping to run into Diana West, who's in town, by the way."

I dropped his hand and pumped the air with my fist. "Yes! I knew it!" Then my lips made an "oh" shape.

He smirked. "And that pretty much tells me the real reason you didn't want me along as your date tonight. Because you thought I'd stop you from confronting a possible criminal."

"Thought?" I looked up at him with a pleading smile. "Does that mean you left Detective Grumpy Pants at home and you're not going to stop me?"

He drew his brows together and scowled deeply, hesitating before finally capitulating. "I'd say this makes us even because you drive me just as crazy with your dangerous impulsive ways." He poked me back, but much softer. "I'm not going to stop you, but don't think for one minute that I'm leaving your side."

I threw myself into his arms and kissed him square on the mouth. He grunted, but his arms came around me and held me tight, kissing me back until I pulled away breathless and slowly slid down the length of him. Let's say his expression was a whole lot sweeter by the time my feet hit the floor. He shook his head with a look that said, *What the hell am I going to do with you?*

"There you are, Sunny, and...oh..." Jo smiled at Mitch, her face flushing. "I didn't expect to see you here, Detective Stone."

"I owe you," he said with conviction, and added sincerely, "I really am sorry, Jo."

"I know." She gave him a hard squeeze. "We'll find the thief. We have to. That's all there is to it."

Cole clapped Mitch on the shoulder. "It wasn't your fault, buddy. But when I get my hands on the person responsible, it ain't gonna be pretty. I'm warning you."

"Duly noted." The detective nodded once. "And for the record, I get first dibs. Those rings went missing on my watch. Not yours. I *will* find out who took them and justice will be served, I can promise you that."

"Good. Now that we're all on the same page, my long lost cousin just arrived." Cole took a step toward the door.

"I'd better handle this, seeing as how I have the most experience, and we don't need you behind bars before your wedding." The detective grabbed his arm to halt him.

"Back off, boys, she's mine." Jo stepped in front of them both.

"Not if I get to her first." I charged past them all.

We all descended upon a tall, dark-haired willowy creature about the same age and the spitting image of Cole, if he had a feminine side, that is. She stepped back, looking startled, but then stood her ground in a ready position, eyeing us warily.

"Wow, if I didn't know better, I would swear you were Cole's twin instead of his cousin," I said, taken aback. I stood there, staring at her in fascination. She even had a couple of tattoos, but somehow they fit and only added to her feminine appeal.

"I've heard that my whole life," she said carefully, still eyeing us all as though we were about to pounce at any moment. "Our mothers were twins, and we look like them."

"Why are you here, Diana?" Jo asked a bit harshly, stepping closer to Cole like a fierce Amazon warrior, ready to pounce on anyone who dared to cause him any more pain. "Those rings don't belong to you."

"Actually, they do. They were supposed to be passed down to all of the women in our family," she said matter-of-factly.

"Is that why you took them?" Mitch asked, pulling out his ever present small notebook and pen. Once a cop always a cop and never completely off duty.

Diana blinked and then frowned. "What do you mean took them? I didn't take anything."

"According to my notes, you arrived in town last night," Mitch said, lifting his gaze to look her in the eye. "That's right. I checked." He had a knack for figuring out if someone was lying or not.

"Goody for you." She threw her hands in the air and looked at us like we were all crazy. "I never said I didn't get in then. What is this all about?"

"Don't play dumb with me, Diana," Cole said with a deep growl. "Grandma's rings are missing, and I want them back."

"You think I took them?" she sputtered, genuine shock registering across her pretty face. "Even though they technically *were* supposed to go to me, I never wanted the rings, Cole. I just said that because you made me mad when you wouldn't listen to me or give me a chance to explain." She shook her head, looking forlorn and hopeless. "Wow, so things are really that bad between us, then?"

Cole frowned with the first hint of doubt shadowing his face. "If you didn't come here for the rings, then what did you come for?"

"You," she said plain and simple and with utmost sincerity.

Jo tugged on his arm until he looked at her. "Babe, you know I'm good at reading people. I think she's telling the truth."

His Adam's apple bobbed, and he looked back at Diana. "Why didn't you come to Gran's funeral?"

It was plain to see Diana was fighting back tears. "Because I didn't know about it. We used to be like brother and sister, Cole. Our mothers were the ones who were at war, but not us. Never us. Unfortunately, Gran chose sides. Lucky for you she chose *your* mother. Mine was never spoken to again. As her daughter, I was guilty by association. I was never notified when she died. When I found out, I was devastated. That's why I reached out to you. You're all I have left. I was hoping we could make our own peace."

We all waited with baited breath, and the silence became unbearable.

Finally Cole cleared his throat and said, "Gran was a hard woman to love, but at the end, she mentioned having a few regrets and wanting to make peace with you, too. I think she would have been proud of the fine woman you've grown into. And I'm sorry I misjudged you. I thought you stayed away on purpose. What do you say we start over?" He held out his hand. "Hi, I'm Cole, the pigheaded idiot who hung up on you."

Diana let out a sob and threw herself into his arms. He stumbled back a step, but then quickly wrapped his big burly arms around her and held on tight. Jo jumped into the middle, wrapping her arms around them both. Mitch blinked a couple of times, his eyes looking misty as a tender smile tipped up the corners of his lips while he looked at the happy trio.

Don't get me wrong, I was happy for all of them as well, but I couldn't stop the worrisome thought from hammering my brain. If Diana West didn't steal the heirloom rings, then that could only mean one thing. While we might have bridged some family ties, we still had a thief in our midst....

And the wedding was still very much on hold!

4

"Father Moody gave a lovely service today, don't you think?" Granny Gert asked while sitting on the wrought-iron bench next to the old-fashioned brass lantern as she broke off pieces of some special cookies she made just for the swans in Mini-Central Park. Granny had a cookie for everything and stored them in her original orange pumpkin cookie jar with the foil covered plate for a lid, swearing that cookies didn't taste the same stored in anything else.

The park was situated in the center of town, just down the street from Sacred Heart Church on Mystical Drive. Ever since she'd driven my Bug off the road and nearly into the pond when I was teaching her to drive, she'd fallen in love with the swans, nicknaming them Fred and Ginger. Every Sunday, rain or snow or shine or heat wave as the case may be right now, we walked to the park after church and fed the swans.

"It was very nice as always," I responded, fanning my heated cheeks, praying for a break in the temperatures to come soon. It was barely past noon and hot as the dickens, not a cloud in the sky.

The swans started trumpeting and flapping their

wings like they did every time they saw my granny. She clapped her hands, bobbing her plastic rain-cap covered head to the beat and humming along. It didn't matter if there wasn't even a remote possibility that it would rain, she wasn't about to take chances with her perfectly curled and set snow white hair getting ruined.

She reached into her faded floral apron made out of flour sacks from years ago—Granny reused everything, adhering to waste not want not, and poor Morty paid the price with his bowties made out of old curtains—and tossed a piece of cookie to Ginger. Granny never went anywhere without her apron. Fred tried to gobble it up first, and Granny tsked, pointing her bony arthritic finger at him in a scolding way. "Ladies first, Fred." Ginger ruffled her feathers, and Fred let out another noisy honk until Granny finally threw him a piece.

"So, are Mom and Dad all set with their reservations at Divine Inspiration?" I asked, still frustrated with Jo for inviting them, but my mother had been a big help in planning her wedding and Jo liked her.

My mother was a well-known ruthless lawyer with impeccable tastes and my father was a renowned cardiologist with a stubborn streak back in New York City. I knew they loved me, and I loved them as well, but *liking* them was a whole different story. It was kind of hard to like people who tried to control my every move and thought I was crazy. No matter how many times I predicted something that they couldn't explain, they were still non-believers. Things hadn't been much better since I'd moved out of their house and made a life for myself in Divinity, but we were working on it.

I just didn't want to "work" on it too frequently.

"Oh, things will work out just fine. They always do. That Theodore fellow doesn't care much for your mother and her demands, but he sure does love my cookies, bless his heart." She winked. "Now if we can just get her to stop telling him how to run his Inn, everything will be peachy keen. Speaking of family, I think it's just wonderful that Cole reunited with his cousin. Diana is a doll. They looked so sweet all sitting together in church today right beside Captain Walker. Do you think Grady noticed my new dress?" She flushed, all atwitter.

I smiled. Captain Grady Walker was much younger than Granny Gert, but that didn't stop her from outrageously flirting with him every chance she got. Sometimes I suspected he was just humoring her by flirting back, but other times I had to wonder. Granny had always been a striking woman with her snow white hair and snappy brown eyes. A petite dynamo with a heart of gold and an ever-present smile on her face. You couldn't help but be happy in her presence.

"You look lovely today," I said and meant it.

She beamed. "Raoulle did a wonderful job with my hair this time down at Pump up the Volume. Tracy did a good job for you and Jo, too. She has a gift, you know. Everyone says so. Why, I heard Lulubelle and Wanda saying that very same thing." She hesitated a beat, and I could see she was dying to tell me something more. "That's not the only thing they were saying, not that I like to spread gossip or anything, mind you."

Lulu was the queen of gossip and our resident Bunco Babe. If anything was going down in Divinity, she knew about it. But she had a heart as big as her cherubic cheeks and triple chins. That's why I couldn't understand what she'd been doing with Wanda the witch, who had the features of a rat and was just as mean. I could tell Granny was chomping at the bit for me to pull it out of her.

"Were they getting their hair done on Friday? I hadn't noticed. So, how is Wanda these days?" I kept the conversation going rather than coming right out and asking Granny to spread the news, which somehow made it acceptable for her to do so, in her eyes anyway.

"Poor Wanda. Zeb's not an easy man to be married to, but lately he's been a bear. I think that's why she walks around with her face so pinched all the time. Maybe I'll give her the latest gossip magazine. They have a miracle cream that's supposed to smooth out the skin and flatten those nasty wrinkles without scary needles and that Bobox stuff."

Granny lived for Friday's at the salon. She was obsessed with the tabloids and believed in every new trend as though it were gospel. "It's Botox, and I don't think a cream is going to change her features, Granny. She looks just like her father. The poor woman got stuck with the wrong set of genes," I replied.

"Well, now sweetie, I don't think new jeans are going to help." She patted my hand with her brown spotted one as if I were the slow one, but then her brow puckered. "Unless you think they're too tight. Maybe she should buy a looser pair so more oxygen can get to her face. I think you're onto something. We'll just puff her up a bit with air. I'm going to write to that magazine and tell them our idea," she said all excited like. "Oh my stars, we'll be famous and puffed air will be the next big thing. Imagine that."

I was imaging that, and the image in my mind's eye

wasn't pretty. "You do that, Granny. In the meantime, why do you think Zeb Erwin is such a bear lately?"

"Because of Cole, of course," she said without missing a beat. She threw out more cookies to a not-so-patiently waiting Fred and Ginger, who honked away in irritation. Granny laughed. "Look, they're serenading me. How sweet."

More like they were letting her have a piece of their mind. "Wait, what?" I asked as her words registered.

"They're singing, silly."

"Not that. What you said before about Cole."

"Oh that." Granny dusted her hands on her apron. "Wanda was telling Lulu that Cole beat Zeb out of that big construction job for a new community center in town. Zeb's business has been around twice as long as Cole's, yet Cole is more savvy and has found ways to cut costs without cutting quality. I guess he felt that job should have been his, and rumor has it they're hurting for money, poor things. Wanda isn't too happy because she has to hear him gripe about it all day. She even said he vowed to get what he deserved one way or another."

I frowned. "And what exactly do you think he meant by that?"

She shrugged. "I don't know, but I *do* know her ears perked right up when Jo was talking about those priceless heirloom rings of Cole's and asking you to store them at your place." Granny winked, and I swear she knew a whole lot more than she let on to people.

"I am such an idiot. I told Jo to bring them over Saturday morning right in front of the whole salon. Anyone could have heard me, but especially someone with a grudge against Cole. Either Wanda or Zeb could have shown up and waited for the perfect moment to strike." I jumped to my feet. "Thanks, Granny, you're the best."

"Well, goodness gracious me," her cheeks turned rosy with pleasure, but then she blinked at me, "where on earth are you going in such a hurry?"

"Shopping. Are you going to be okay here alone?"

"Oh, fiddledeedee, I can take care of myself, you silly girl. Been doing it long before you were alive. It's a beautiful day. I'll just finish up here and walk back to the church then drive myself home to start dinner. I'm more worried about you. Scary things happen when you get that crazed look in your eyes, young lady."

I just smiled and wiggled my eyebrows at her and then took off running. People *should* be scared when I got this way. Crazy with a capital C is what I became when people messed with my friends, and right now the Erwins should be very afraid.

I made it to Perry's Pawn shop before it closed, totally out of breath and sweaty and irritable. I really hated to exercise. Wally down at Wally's World was still on a mission to make me a believer. I was a believer, all right. A believer in not exerting any more energy than I had to. Okay, fine, I was lazy, plain and simple.

"Miss Meadows, what a pleasure to see you." Perry LaLone grinned wide, his black hair slicked back, his capped teeth pearly white, and his smile as phony as ever. He wasn't a bad guy, just cheesy and cheap and always out for himself.

"Pleasure to see you too, Mr. LaLone." I smiled back just as wide, not completely unskilled in playing the game.

"How's that charming grandmother of yours?"

"She's doing well, thanks. But I'm not here for small talk, Perry. I'm here to do business." I rested my hands on the counter and looked around conspiratorially, then leaned in close. "A little birdie told me you got some new merchandise in yesterday." I bluffed.

He raised a brow. "Maybe. Maybe not. What are you in the market for, and I'll let you know."

"Jewelry, and not just any jewelry. I'm looking for something expensive from, oh, let's say a mutual acquaintance with the last name of Erwin."

He blinked, surprised, but then quickly recovered and I could already see the calculator in his brain crunching numbers. "You like to stay informed, I see, but it might cost you...if I even have the merchandise you're looking for."

"Money's no object for something special, and let's just say I need something special for a wedding present."

He walked to the front of his shop, turned the lock and flipped his sign to closed.

"I'm not technically supposed to do a transaction yet since I have to give the seller a chance to change his mind, but for you I just might make an exception. If the price is right, that is." He was practically salivating over the thought of making a hefty profit. I hated to burst his bubble, but I had the law on my side, and I wouldn't have to pay a dime for stolen goods. I would love the chance to return the rings to Cole and Jo and see the looks on their faces.

"I need to see the merchandise first."

"Then follow me, Miss Meadows. Something tells me you won't be disappointed."

Bingo!

5

"Come on in and make yourselves comfortable," Jo said, opening the door wide to their brand new home. A cute little modern ranch with a fenced-in back yard not far from my own. A perfect starter house for a new family with a dog.

Jo and Cole had invited Mitch and I and Morty over to join them for Sunday dinner. "I love what you've done to the place," I said, following her into the kitchen.

"Thanks. It's still a work in progress, but it's coming along."

She opened the back door and we stepped out onto the deck, overlooking the yard. Biff lay sprawled out on the ground and didn't so much as flinch when Morty ran past him and leapt onto the top of his doghouse with a hearty meow.

"What's up with Biff?" Mitch asked.

She shrugged. "Not sure. Animals are like children. They can tell when Mommy and Daddy are upset. He's not himself."

"That makes sense," I said, nodding toward my illustrious cat using the roof of Biff's dog house as a scratching pad. "Morty's been acting weird, too."

"Morty *is* weird," Mitch grumbled, earning a scowl from me that said, *You promised you'd try harder.*

He sighed long and deep.

"Biff will be fine," Cole said. "We all will." He gave Jo a hug and held up two cigars and two longnecks, motioning for Mitch to follow him out into the yard to a pair of Adirondack chairs facing west so they could watch the sunset.

"I'll let you know when I'm ready for you to cook the steaks." Jo grabbed me and pulled me into the kitchen. "So, did you find out anything new?" she asked as she poured us each a frozen margarita. She prepared the baked potatoes while I cut up veggies for a salad.

"As a matter of fact, I did. I thought I had a lead with Zeb Erwin. His wife Wanda overheard us talking at Pump up the Volume on Friday about you bringing the rings over on Saturday morning. Granny said they were hurting for money, and he vowed to get what was coming to him because he lost out on the community center bid to Cole."

"You don't think they would stoop that low, do you?"

"Actually I did. I thought maybe they were the ones to steal the rings so I went to Perry's Pawn shop. Turns out they did pawn something late Saturday night, but it wasn't the rings. It was his grandfather's watch. Perry wasn't too happy when I passed on buying it after he shut down his shop early just for me."

Her shoulders slumped. "Maybe Zeb just hasn't pawned them yet." She looked at me hopefully.

"Mitch and I thought that too, but why wouldn't he get rid of them as soon as he could? We actually talked to him this afternoon, and he says he and his wife were home on Saturday going over their finances and figuring out what they could pawn. They don't have proof, of course, but I can't think of a good reason for them to hold onto the rings when they are desperate for money."

"Unless he's biding his time because he knows they're stolen goods." Jo set the table as she talked.

"Maybe." I shrugged, grabbing some napkins and helping her. "In the meantime, can you think of anyone else who might want the rings or have something against you and Cole being together?"

"Before yesterday, no," Jo replied. "But now that you mention it, Veronica Lewis quit last night, leaving me high and dry for hired help today. That's why I had to push back dinner tonight. I had to work all day."

"Why would she quit? She's one of your best waitresses. Hasn't she worked for you for years?" I asked.

"She sure has. We go way back. We actually went to high school together. We've never really been friends, but we certainly weren't enemies."

"Then how does this relate to this case?"

"Because Cole and I are together now."

"You mean Veronica has a thing for Cole?"

"Apparently so, but I never knew it. Cole said she's always had a crush on him. They even dated once back in the day. But then he got married, and she was heartbroken. After Cole's wife died, she started coming around, offering to help him. He told her he wasn't ready, but truth is he just didn't feel that way about her any more. She accepted he needed more time, but when he fell for me and asked me to marry him so quickly, she changed toward me. Became cold and aloof. I couldn't figure out why, but she did her job well so I didn't see a reason to fire her."

"Why wouldn't she have quit before now then?" I asked.

"I honestly think she thought we wouldn't last. But she was here Friday night when Cole showed me his grandmother's rings and we talked about taking them over to your house the next day. She must have overheard us. The next day the rings were stolen, and she didn't show up for work that night. She called in first thing this morning and said she quit."

"Did you ask her why?"

"Yes, and all she said was that I didn't deserve her any more than I deserved Cole or his grandmother's rings. Then she said to mark her words, my wedding would be a disaster."

"Wow."

"Do you think she could be right? Is my wedding meant to fail? I heard she was a witch."

"Oh, she's a witch, all right, but not the kind you're worried about. She's just trying to scare you, and I think we just found our next suspect."

The rest of dinner involved the four of us talking about our next plan of attack. When we went to leave, Morty was missing, but that wasn't unusual. Morty had a habit of appearing and disappearing at will, which meant he had gotten bored and was probably already at home. Mitch obviously needed a break, so we headed toward Warm Beginnings and Cozy Endings café for coffee.

"Okay, let's regroup," Mitch said as we pulled into the parking lot. "The thief is obviously not Diana, so we can rule her out."

"And Zeb and Wanda are each other's alibi's, saying they were at home going over finances at the time of the robbery, but they can't prove it," I stated.

"True, but it also wouldn't make sense for them not to pawn the rings for cash if they had them," Mitch added as we climbed out of the car.

"Then all that leaves is Veronica Lewis," I said as we walked inside with Mitch in the lead.

He stopped short, and I bounced off his back. "Speak of the devil," he said.

Veronica wore an apron as she stood behind the counter and filled coffee and dessert orders. She looked up, saw us staring, and her face flushed pink.

"Well, that's a guilty look if ever I saw one," I said from beside Mitch. "And I can tell you for certain that this job doesn't pay nearly as much as Smokey Jo's. So how is Veronica paying her bills? Did she steal the rings and pawn them in another town?"

"Now now," he responded quietly, "innocent until proven otherwise. We both know the importance of not judging someone too quickly."

"True, but we also both saw the looks on Jo and Cole's faces when the rings turned up missing because of us, I might add."

He looked down at me, and raised one thick black brow. "What did you do wrong? I was the one who put the rings on my workbench. It was my responsibility to keep them safe."

"Only because I ordered you to do so." I rested my palms on his chest and said with resolve, "*We* made this mess. *We* need to fix it."

He blew out a breath, and I could tell he wasn't happy about involving me. "Fine, how do you want to handle this? Good cop bad cop?" he asked with a grim expression, and I wondered if I would ever get him to stop worrying so much. Probably not.

"I got dibs on good cop." I smirked, trying to lighten the mood. I patted his chest and stepped in front to lead the way, adding over my shoulder, "You couldn't be good if you tried."

6

"I hate to say it, but I think it's time to throw in the towel," Jo said sadly through the phone on Monday morning.

"You can't give up, Jo," I replied pleadingly. Mitch and I had grilled Veronica, but she claimed she went for a hike in the trails around the park to clear her head Saturday morning, and she came to the realization that she couldn't work for Jo any longer. She needed to quit in order to move on and get over Cole. Of course she didn't have an alibi, either, which gave me hope. "Veronica could still be guilty. Mitch is looking into her more closely as we speak."

"Finding the guilty culprit could take weeks, Sunny. Our wedding is right around the corner. While I would love to wear Cole's grandmother's heirloom rings, I can't risk not having any rings at all. I already feel like my wedding is doomed for some reason. I don't want to rock the boat any further. Can you watch Biff while Cole and I go ring shopping? I feel bad leaving him alone. I know you have clients, so I can bring him over to your house. He'll be fine outside."

"Sure thing," I replied, feeling awful that we hadn't been successful in getting the rings back. It just felt wrong for Cole and Jo to buy a new set, but I understood her nervousness. I had always believed in signs, but I also knew for certain that Jo and Cole were meant to be together. "Your wedding is not doomed. This is just a hiccup. Everything will work out. You'll see," I said reassuringly, yet even I wasn't convinced nothing would go wrong.

"I hope so." She tried to sound positive. "See you in a few minutes."

We hung up, and I gave a reading for the mayor, one of my best clients. When I finished, he left and I puppy proofed the house, getting ready for Biff. I gave Morty a stern lecture to behave, and then Jo arrived. She dropped Biff off and then went to meet Cole, looking anything but excited over what should be one of the happiest moments of her life—picking out the rings that would symbolize their love.

Lightning streaked across the sky and then thunder boomed a few minutes later, creating an ominous foreboding atmosphere. The universe wasn't any happier with the situation than I was, but what could I do? I only hoped Mitch could find something incriminating on Veronica or Zeb or Wanda in time. My next client cancelled, and Granny was busy inside cleaning because it was Monday. Granny never veered from her schedule. I stepped outside, and Biff sat there like an angel. A little sadder than normal, but an angel nonetheless.

"I know how you feel, buddy," I said as I looked up at the sky, knowing it was about to open up and rain hard. Weird because the sun had been out a moment ago, and the forecast didn't call for rain.

Morty appeared by my side and stared at me.

"Come on, boy. It's going to rain. Let's go inside." I went to pick him up, but he scurried out of my way, further into the yard. "Morty, what's gotten into you? You are being very naughty. This is not the time to play games." I chased after him, but he kept slipping just out of my reach, with an amused expression on his haughty face. "Fine, have it your way. But when you come in looking like a drowned rat, I don't want to hear one single hiss. Understood?"

I swear to God he rolled his eyes at me.

"Why can't you be a good boy like Biff?" Shaking my head, I went to gather up a much bigger yet infinitely easier target, leaving Morty to fend for himself. That would teach him.

Biff wagged his tail as I drew closer. I started to pick up his toys so I'd have everything together when Jo returned, but when I picked up his bone, I froze. My eyes narrowed into tunnel vision like they always did during a reading, and suddenly I was looking out of the eyes of the thief. The thief must have had Biff's bone at some point and then the poor baby must have witnessed the whole thing, I realized. No wonder he was out of sorts. He'd been through so much before being adopted by Cole and Jo, but he was doing tons better. Poor guy probably wanted to give back to them by telling them who the guilty culprit was, but he couldn't talk.

My thoughts faded as the eyes I stared out of crouched low to the ground, watching Mitch and Cole come out of the garage. It must have been right after Mitch had put the rings on his workbench. I was surprised we hadn't heard Biff barking. Then again, Cole took Biff everywhere. The dog knew everyone in town, so the thief obviously wasn't a stranger.

The guys went inside, and then the thief didn't waste a single moment before bolting to the garage. They ran really fast so it had to be someone young and energetic, which pretty much ruled out Zeb. Wanda was in decent shape, but I was leaning more toward Veronica who jogged regularly. I couldn't tell what was happening, like maybe the thief struggled with the door, but finally got it open. Then the person tore through the place in such a hurry I couldn't make out what was going on. The thief was probably afraid of getting caught because they were breathing heavy and I could feel their heart beating wildly.

I frowned. Maybe the thief couldn't see that well because it looked like they literally stuck their head all over the place, right next to each item, inspecting it closely. Above things, below things, shaking things, and then finally grabbing the bag of rings with their...

I sucked in a breath, dropped the bone, and my jaw grew slack. As quickly as I could, I grabbed my phone and called Jo.

"What's up?" she asked.

"Did you buy the rings yet?" I blurted, panting.

"Um, no, are you all right? You sound like you're ready to hyperventilate."

"I'm fine, I'm fine. Just, don't buy new rings!"

"Okay, why? What on earth has gotten into you?"

"I found your thief. Don't ask. Just get here now!" I hung up, knowing that would spur her to move. I made a call to Mitch and told him the same message, then hung up on him as well. I had to laugh when they all showed up within minutes, probably breaking every speeding record imaginable.

Meanwhile Morty was still evading me and the thunder and lightning were getting louder and closer.

Jo and Cole ran into the back yard, followed quickly by Mitch who nearly ran over them both with gun drawn and eyes wide. They all looked around and spoke at the same time:

"Who's the thief?"

"Did they get away?"

"Should I call backup?"

"Put your phone away, Detective, and holster that weapon. No they didn't get away, Cole. And Jo, your wedding is not doomed, but your parenting skills might be."

"What are you talking about, Tink, because once again you're not making a whole lot of sense? And right about now I'm ready to trade places and put *you* in the doghouse for scaring the hell out of me." Mitch scowled.

"Let's just say I had a vision and saw the whole thing. Very creepy. Hiding out near the woods, watching us, then breaking into the garage and trashing the place. But what finally gave away who the thief is was when he put the rings in his mouth to carry them out."

"*His* mouth?" Cole rubbed his jaw.

"Are you saying what I think you're saying?" Jo asked, while narrowing her eyes and turning her stare on her dog, who blinked at us innocently.

"Exactly. Turns out Biff isn't such a *good boy* after all." I glanced at Morty, who rolled his eyes at me with a look that said *Duh!* and finally went inside. The sky suddenly cleared, the sun came back out, and I realized what he'd been trying to tell me all along. "I'm thinking Biff was still jealous of you taking Cole away from him, so he grabbed the rings and hid them."

"So that's why Morty was digging up the yard," Mitch said. "I thought he was the one who put all the holes there."

"He was probably just trying to find the rings, knowing Biff had hidden them all along. He even scratched on Biff's doghouse, yet none of us picked up on it." Cole turned disappointed eyes on Biff, who whined pathetically and covered his face with his massive paw.

Cole was the angry one this time, and Jo actually softened, coming to Biff's rescue. "Awww, he's just a baby, Daddy." She walked over to the Great Dane who was so big already it was scary to imagine what he would look like fully grown. Kneeling by his side, she rubbed him behind the ears and then kissed his nose. "He didn't mean any harm. He just loves his daddy. I do too, buddy, and like it or not, you're stuck with us both because I love you too." Her words earned her huge brownie points as a mommy in Biff's eyes, judging by the adoring looks he was sending her and the kisses he landed on her cheeks. She laughed and Cole couldn't help but grin.

"Now, the key is getting him to show us where they are," I said. "I kind of dropped the bone after I realized it was him. I'm guessing he buried them in a hole, though."

"Gee, ya think." Mitch laughed. "Whatever gave you the clue, Watson?"

I frowned. "Watch it, Grumpy Pants. You're not out of the doghouse yet."

EPILOGUE

"Come on, Tink. I can't possibly still be in the doghouse?" Mitch asked one week later as he joined me on the back deck that looked out over the yard.

After literally digging up the entire yard, we'd finally found Cole's grandmother's heirloom wedding rings. They weren't in a hole at all. They were hidden in my flower beds, right where Morty had been looking the first day. I think Biff had been deciding where he was going to bury his bone when he dug the holes, never intending to bury the rings in the first place, the naughty boy.

I sighed. "No, you're not in the doghouse anymore, Grump Butt." I smiled up at him and scooted over to make room on the glider. "You did a great job filling the holes, replanting the grass and fixing the flowers. The yard should be just about perfect by the time I have Jo's wedding shower." My mother had wanted it at a classy restaurant instead of my deathtrap of an ancient house with my creepy cat, of course, but I had wanted to have the shower my way at my house. And Jo, sensing I needed to help in at least some way, agreed.

Mitch slid his arm around me, and I rested my head on his shoulder. "It'll be amazing, you know," he said softly.

"I hope so. I'm the maid of honor, but it feels more like my mother is. I hate competing with her in this way."

"She wants to feel needed, that's all, so Jo's letting her help with the small details. But you're the one she leans on for emotional support when those pre-wedding jitters creep in."

"I guess," I said, feeling better.

"I know," he said tenderly.

"How?"

"Because I know you. And *you're* amazing." He leaned down and kissed me softly, and I melted into him.

"Any regrets," he asked after pulling away, and I knew he meant about him moving in with me.

"Not a single one. You?"

"None." Morty appeared out of nowhere as usual, and Mitch startled then chuckled. "I'll never get used to that, but we've come to a real truce of sorts."

"I know." I winked.

"How?" He blinked.

"See where he's standing?" I pointed.

Mitch eyed me curiously, then looked at my cat. "Yeah?"

"What's missing that should be there?"

He thought about it for a minute, then a light dawned in his eyes and he snapped his fingers. "No shadow. He's standing there with the setting sun shining right on him, yet there's no shadow. What does that mean?"

My smile came slow and sweet, and for the first

time since Mitch had moved in, I truly relaxed as I replied, "That the shenanigans are finally over."

The End

Coming Soon!
Perish in the Palm (a Sunny Meadows Mystery) -
NOVEL - June 2015
Hazard in the Horoscope (a Sunny Meadows Mystery)
- NOVEL - Sept 2015

ACKNOWLEDGMENTS

As always to my amazing husband, Brian. You keep life interesting and fun. And to the rest of my children: Josh, Matt and Emily. You make life joyful. And to my extended family: the Harmons, the Russos and the Townsends. And to my critique partner, Barbara Witek, who truly is a goddess! And to Dar Albert, who rocks at covers! And last but never least, to my fabulous agent Christine Witthohn of Book Cents Literary Agency. Love you, doll!

ABOUT THE AUTHOR

Kari Lee Townsend is a National Bestselling Author of mysteries & a tween superhero series. She also writes romance and women's fiction as Kari Lee Harmon. With a background in English education, she's now a full-time writer, wife to her own superhero, mom of 3 sons, 1 darling diva, 1 daughter-in-law & 2 lovable fur babies. These days you'll find her walking her dogs or hard at work on her next story, living a blessed life.

ALSO BY THE AUTHOR

Printed in the USA
CPSIA information can be obtained
at www.ICGtesting.com
LVHW030845300624
784301LV00034B/1326